REAMONN WISH

SONGS & SPECIALS

IMPRESSUM

Die in diesem Buch enthaltenen Songs sind alle urheberrechtlich geschützt.
Nachdruck nur mit Genehmigung der Verfügungsberechtigten erlaubt.

Text und Musik:
Garvey, Gommeringer, Bossert, Rauenbusch, Padotzke.

Herausgeber:
reamonn publishing / b612 publishing.

Alle Rechte an der Zusammenstellung dieses Buches liegen bei Reamonn.
www.reamonn.de, www.reamonn.com

Reamonn sind:
Rea Garvey, Mike „Gomezz" Gommeringer, Uwe Bossert,
Philipp Rauenbusch, Sebastian Padotzke

Vielen Dank an Frank Schmidt für den Notensatz,
Olaf Heine, Olli Look und Rea Garvey für die Fotos,
excogito designkonzepte für das Layout und das
Seitendesign, Dirk Rudolph für das Artwork,
Christof Schulte für das Coverfoto und
Duncan Ó Ceallaigh für die Übersetzung ins Englische.

© 2006 Reamonn

IMPRINT

All the songs in this book are copyrighted material. Copying of all or any
sections of this book is allowed with the permission of the copyright holders.

All songs written by
Garvey, Gommeringer, Bossert, Rauenbusch, Padotzke.

Published by
reamonn publishing / b612 publishing.

All rights for this book held by Reamonn.
www.reamonn.de, www.reamonn.com

Reamonn are:
Rea Garvey, Mike „Gomezz" Gommeringer, Uwe Bossert,
Philipp Rauenbusch, Sebastian Padotzke

Many thanks to Frank Schmidt for the notation,
Olaf Heine, Olli Look and Rea Garvey for the photos,
excogito designkonzepte for the layout and
additional design, Dirk Rudolph for the artwork,
Christof Schulte for the cover photo and
Duncan Ó Ceallaigh for the English translation.

© 2006 Reamonn

INHALT / CONTENTS

VORWORT

Die folgenden Worte sollen euch einen kleinen Einblick in die Entstehung unseres Albums „Wish" gewähren. Alles zu erzählen, was wir während dieser Zeit erlebt haben, würde sicher den Rahmen dieses Buches sprengen. Daher beschränke ich mich auf wenige Zeilen, wenn das für einen Schlagzeuger überhaupt möglich ist ;-). Nichtsdestotrotz hoffe ich, ihr habt etwas Spaß beim Lesen. Falls ihr mehr wissen wollt, könnt ihr uns ja beim nächsten Konzert, Fantreffen oder einer anderen Gelegenheit persönlich fragen ...

Fotografie: Olaf Heine

Als unser Songwriting für den Nachfolger von „Beautiful Sky" schon recht fortgeschritten war, machten wir uns Gedanken mit wem wir das Album aufnehmen könnten. Wir hatten mit einigen Produzenten Kontakt aufgenommen und ein paar Treffen organisiert, um die Leute persönlich kennen zu lernen, u. a. flogen wir eines Tages nach Los Angeles, um uns mit Greg Fidelman zusammen zu setzen. Nach ein paar Minuten hatten alle am Tisch ein Lächeln im Gesicht, und eines war uns klar: Greg ist unser Mann. Er hatte die gleiche Vision für das Album wie wir. Greg schlug vor, das Ganze in L.A. stattfinden zu lassen. Hier wüsste er genau, wo und wie er das Beste für und aus uns herausholen könne. Darüber mussten wir erstmal kurz nachdenken: Kalifornien, Sonne, Strand und Meer ist ja nicht unbedingt jedermanns Ding, oder!

FOREWORD

What follows will hopefully allow you to gain some insight into how our album 'Wish' came to be. To tell of everything that happened during that time would exceed the scope of what this book is about, so I've tried to keep things short and sweet - if such a thing is possible for a drummer ;-). Nevertheless I hope you enjoy what you read. Should there be anything else that you want to know, then use the next opportunity, whether it is the next gig, fan convention or whatever, to ask us personally...

It was as the songwriting for the follow up to 'Beautiful Sky' was in a fairly advanced stage that we started to think about with whom we could go and record the new album. We had contacted a number of producers and organized a couple of meetings in order to get to know those concerned personally. Amongst these appointments was a flight to L.A. to see Greg Fidelman. It took just a couple of minutes into the meeting before everyone was smiling and one thing had already become clear: Greg is our man. He shared the same vision we had for the album. It was Greg who suggested that everything should take place in L.A. – there he knew exactly where and how he could get the best for and from us. We had to think that one over a bit... after all, California, sun, sea, beaches – it's not everybody's thing. But sometimes it's necessary to make sacrifices for one's art ;-) Once everything had been settled (which dates, studio and accommodation we could get) we found ourselves at the end of August 2005 flying over to Los Angeles for a stay of just under 4 months. After quickly settling in it was right off to the rehearsal space. It was quite away out of town and from outside it looked nothing special at all. However once inside, our room was very rock'n'roll, decked out to create just the right mood. The whole complex was pretty crazy, and it turned out that several big names had rehearsed there (David Bowie being just one). The time we spent there was both very exciting and very productive.

Naja, aber man muss eben manchmal Opfer bringen :-). Nachdem alles geklärt war (Zeitraum, welches Studio, welche Unterkunft usw.), ging es also Ende August 2005 für knapp 4 Monate nach Los Angeles. Dort angekommen haben wir uns nach einer kurzen Eingewöhnungszeit direkt in den Proberaum begeben. Etwas außerhalb gelegen, sah das Gebäude recht unscheinbar aus. Unser Raum war jedoch sehr rock'n'rollig und sorgte für die passende Stimmung. Der ganze Komplex an sich war sehr kultig. Hier haben schon etliche Größen (wie z. B. David Bowie) geprobt. Die Zeit hier war wirklich sehr produktiv und spannend.

Wir haben sechs Tage die Woche von morgens bis abends konzentriert an unseren Ideen und Songs gearbeitet. Gestört wurden wir manchmal nur von Audioslave, die direkt neben uns probten und deren Bassgewitter bei uns so präsent war, dass wir lautstärkemäßig auch etwas nachlegen mussten. Aber ansonsten waren die Jungs ganz nett :-). Nachdem diese Phase abgeschlossen war, ging es direkt ins Sound City Studio zum Aufnehmen. Die Liste der Künstler, die hier schon gearbeitet haben, ist lang (u. a. Johnny Cash und Nirvana). Hier wurde auf jeden Fall schon Musikgeschichte geschrieben, und wir wollten einen kleinen Teil dazu beitragen. Wie sagte die Studiomanagerin immer so schön: „Go and make some history." Unser Plan war, die Basic Sachen alle zusammen in einem Raum live einzuspielen. Dies war uns sehr wichtig, nachdem wir bei „Dream No. 7" und „Beautiful Sky" erst Drums und dann nach und nach den Rest eingespielt haben, was wir damals auch alle für gut befunden hatten. Auf „Wish" wollten wir wieder mehr Live-Feeling. Dies bedeutete für uns, jeden Song so oft zu spielen, bis wir das Gefühl hatten, das Wesentliche auf Band gebracht zu haben. Dabei ging es uns weniger um Perfektion, sondern eher darum, den magischen Moment einzufangen. Eine leicht verstimmte Gitarre, ein etwas daneben gegangener Snareschlag oder Ähnliches waren uns

We spent six days a week from mornings until evenings concentrating on our ideas and songs. The only disturbance there came in the form of Audioslave, who occasionally rehearsed directly next door. Their thunderous bass action was almost omnipresent, leaving us no other option but to even things out in terms of loudness! That aside, the lads themselves were pretty cool :-)

Once the rehearsal phase was over, we went directly into Sound City Studio to record. The list of artists that had recorded there was a long one - Johnny Cash and Nirvana being just two examples. It was no exaggeration to say that music history had been made here, and now we wanted to contribute our little bit to it. As the studio manager always put it so well, "Go and make some history." Our plan was to lay down the basic backing tracks live, all of us playing in one room. This was very important to us, as for "Dream No. 7" and "Beautiful Sky" we had recorded the drums first and then played the rest over the top. We had found that worked for us then, but on "Wish" we wanted to go back to a more live feeling. This meant playing any given song as often as it took to get what we felt was its essence onto tape. The aim had less to do with attaining perfection as capturing that 'magical moment'. Something like a slightly out-of-tune guitar or a slightly late snare hit was not a problem if what we heard felt good. As soon as the red light went on in

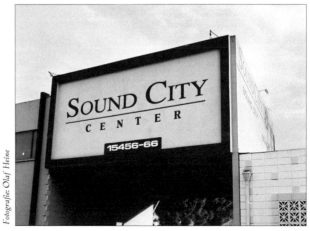

Fotografie Olaf Heine

kein Dorn im Auge, wenn sich das, was wir hörten, gut anfühlte. Sobald in der Regie die rote Lampe anging und von Greg der Satz „It sounds like a record to me" ertönte, war in der Regel unser Ziel erreicht. Nach Beendigung der Basics ging es an die Overdubs. Aus rein trommeltechnischer Sicht durfte ich in dieser Zeit mein zweites persönliches „Wish"-Highlight erleben. Aber vielleicht sollte ich dazu kurz das erste erwähnen. Erstmals hatten wir einen Drum Tech mit im Studio dabei. Das war nicht irgendwer, sondern Lee Smith, der unter anderem schon für den richtigen Studioschlagzeugsound bei den Red Hot Chili Peppers gesorgt hatte. Der Mann kann etliche Geschichten und Anekdoten erzählen. Ich habe ihm auf jeden Fall gern zugehört und auch einige Fragen gestellt. Mein zweites Highlight waren die Percussionaufnahmen. Hier gab es dieses Mal einen Gastmusiker. Greg fragte mich, ob ich etwas dagegen hätte, wenn jemand anderes Percussion spielen würde. Als dann der Name Lenny Castro fiel, meinte ich nur, dass es mir eine Ehre sei, wenn Lenny auf unserem Album spielen würde. An dieser Stelle muss ich vielleicht erwähnen, dass Mr. Castro bereits auf vielen legendären Alben und für etliche Größen gespielt hat. Ihm bei der Arbeit zuzusehen war einfach großartig. Er war sehr angetan von meinem Spiel und ich von seinem. Natürlich hab ich auch wieder einige interessante Geschichten zu hören bekommen. Schlagwerker unter sich ... :-) Nachdem alle Aufnahmen abgeschlossen waren, ging es zum Mischen ins Sound Factory Studio, und für uns wurde es etwas entspannter. Zumindest glaubten wir das anfangs noch ...

Es gab da noch einen Song, den wir alle sehr mochten, bei dem wir aber das Gefühl hatten, dass er in seiner derzeitigen Form nicht zum Rest des Albums passte. Deswegen hatten wir ihn erstmal auf Eis gelegt. Dann bekamen wir Besuch von unserer Plattenfirma und unserem Management. Die waren von der Nummer derart begeistert und

Fotografie: Olaf Heine

the control room and Greg uttered the sentence "it sounds like a record to me", in most cases it meant we had achieved our goal. Once the backing tracks were finished we moved onto the overdubs. From a purely technical drumming standpoint it was then that I had the chance to enjoy my second 'Wish' highlight. But perhaps I should mention the first one beforehand. For the first time we had a drum technician in the studio – not just anyone either, but Lee Smith, who had been responsible for getting the right drum sound for amongst others the Red Hot Chili Peppers. This was a guy with endless stories and anecdotes to tell, and I for one, was more than glad to listen and ask questions. Anyway, back to the second highlight, which turned out to be the percussion recordings. This time around we had invited a guest musician in. Greg had asked me if I was cool with getting someone else in to play percussion. When the name Lenny Castro was mentioned I could only reply that it would be an honour to have him play on our album. For the record I should perhaps mention that Mr. Castro has played on a multitude of legendary albums by an equal number of big names. Watching him play was simply fantastic. He enthused about my playing and vice-versa. Of course I also got to hear a lot more interesting stories... but get two beatmakers together and you shouldn't expect anything else :-)

wünschten sich, dass wir den Song doch noch auf Band bringen. Daraufhin haben wir im Mixing-studio in einem Nebenraum unser Equipment erneut aufgebaut und die Arbeit an dem Stück wieder aufgenommen. Greg war mit dem Mischen beschäftigt und kam ab und zu zu uns rüber, um zu sehen, ob wir vorwärts kamen, und wir schauten bei ihm rein, um seine Fortschritte zu hören. Das zog sich einige Tage so hin, bis der Moment kam, in dem wir uns alle einig waren: Der Song ist zur Aufnahme bereit. Dafür verfrachteten wir unser Equipment rüber in das zweite, von uns bis dahin noch nicht belegte Studio der Sound Factory. Wir haben die Nummer einige Male gespielt und als dann wieder der Satz „It sounds like a record to me" fiel, waren wir alle happy. Die Aufnahmen für den Song wurden im wahrsten Sinne des Wortes auf dem letzten Drücker fertig. Kaum war der fina-le Ton verklungen, waren die ersten von uns schon Richtung Heimat unterwegs. Ein paar Tage später war auch der Rest von uns wieder in Deutschland angekommen.

P.S.: Bei dem Song, der es fast nicht aufs Album geschafft hätte, handelt es sich um „Tonight".
Gomezz

Once the recordings had been completed it was on to mixing - also at Sound Factory Studio - with the difference that for us things would be a little more relaxed. At least that's what we believed at first...

There was one song that we all really liked but which we felt in its current shape didn't really fit the rest of the album. So initially we put it on ice and moved on. Then we received a visit from both our management and label. They were so knocked out by the track that they insisted we try and get the song onto the album. To this end we set up our equipment in a room adjacent to the mixing studio and set about recording it again. Greg was taken up with mixing and so he would come across every once in a while to see how we were coming long, and then we'd saunter across to hear what progress he was making with the mixes. This went on for a couple of days until we unanimously agreed the song was ready to record. Our equipment was then transferred to the second (and luckily available) studio in Sound Factory, which we hadn't until that point used before. We played the number a num-ber of times and as the magic sentence "it sounds like a record to me" finally came, we were all happy. The recording for the song went right down to the final deadline – it was touch and go. Hardly had the last notes faded out before a couple of us had to make our way back home to Germany, followed by the rest a couple of days later.

P.S.: For the curious amongst you out there, the song I referred to above was in fact 'Tonight'.
Gomezz

Fotografie: Olaf Heine

Fotografie Olaf Heine

This is my personal favourite song on the album everyone in the band has a different favourite but this mine! The song describes for me a way of life, "don't give up because you have every-thing to loose". The song talks about keeping the dream alive, everyone of us has had a childhood dream and somewhere along the way we loose our grip on it, we need to believe sometimes that the impossible is possible. My parents have 8 kids and were the only ones who truly believed that I could succeed as a musician even sometimes more than myself, my mum is a great believer in playing the cards you've been dealt, no moaning no self pity in her own words "keep the head down and get on with it". They gave me enough room in my life for dreams and enough support in my life to follow them. *Rea*

Fotografie: Olaf Heine

WISH

♩ = ca. 66

Intro & Interlude

guitar

% *Vers*

1. see the sun   shine a - bove your head   see the love   that you once
2. see the dreams   that you hold in - side   see the hope   see the co -
3. see the world   through a child's eyes   ne - ver give up   or let it

had   don't e - ver let   go   oh no   don't e - ver let
lours fly   don't e - ver let   go   oh no   don't e - ver let
slip by   don't e - ver let   go   oh no   don't e - ver let

3. don't e - ver let go   when for - tune o - pens wide

go
go
go

oh no
oh no

Chorus

and if you wish u - pon it   with
yeah if you wish u - pon it   you'll

o - pen eyes   the world will sing to you_____
be sur - prised   how the world will sing to you_____

BASS

Pick, Fender Precision, Flat-Wound-Saiten

Ich habe „Wish" mit einem Fender Precision (frühes 70er Modell), Flatwound-Saiten (45 auf 105er Stärke) und Pick eingespielt.

Achtung: Das G soll auf der E-Saite im 15. Bund gegriffen werden – dieser Ton wird leicht zu laut, soll aber ganz harmonisch in die Linie integriert werden. *Philipp Rauenbusch*

I played 'Wish' with an early 70's Fender Precision, using flat wound strings (45 – 105 gauge) and a plectrum.

By the way: the G on the 15th fret of the E string should be fingered – the tone will be slightly too loud, but should be integrated nicely into the line. *Philipp Rauenbusch*

Fotografie: Olaf Heine

Schon der Album-Opener „Wish" – mein absoluter Lieblingssong – hat im Intro einen relativ komplexen Gitarrensound. Ich bin oft gefragt worden, was das ist, ob er mehrere Gitarren oder vielleicht Unterstützung von einem Keyboard erhält. Hier die Auflösung: es ist eine Gitarre mit einem „Reverse Delay", ich habe hier den genialen line6-dl4 verwendet. Ist alles eine Gitarre und Sebi`s Toypiano, das mit seinem glasklaren Ton mit der Gitarre die Melodie spielt.

Wenn ihr richtig in die Boxen eurer Stereoanlage reinkriecht, hört ihr auf der linken Seite einen ganz leisen Sound, klingt ein bisschen wie eine Grille, die einen Hänger hat. Das sind zwei Töne von meiner Gitarre, die ich aufgenommen habe und jeden einzelnen Ton dann im Computer rumgedreht habe. War 'ne Höllenarbeit, aber macht einen geilen Sound, den man nicht mit Spielen hinbekommt. *Uwe Bossert*

The album opener 'Wish' – my absolute favourite by the way – uses a relatively complex guitar sound in its intro. I'm often asked whether I use a number of layered guitars or if perhaps there's a keyboard underneath; the answer is, it's one guitar with a 'reverse delay' from the truly excellent Line6 dl4 pedal, with the crystal clear sound Sebi's toy piano doubling on the melody.

If you get right close up to your stereo speakers, you'll hear on the left channel a very quiet sound; something a bit like a cricket. It is in fact two notes from guitar that I recorded individually and then messed about with on the computer. It was nitpicky work, but it's a cool sound that you wouldn't otherwise be able to play. *Uwe Bossert*

Die Melodie am Anfang des Songs unisono mit Gitarre ist auf einem Jaymar Kinderpiano aus den 70er Jahren gespielt. Ich hatte das kleine Klavier in einem Secondhandladen auf dem Sunset gefunden und wollte es eigentlich nur als Souvenir für meine kleine Tochter mitnehmen. Im Studio klimperte ich drauf rum und Greg war so begeistert von dem Sound, dass er es gleich aufnehmen wollte.
Sebastian Padotzke

The melody at the beginning of the song is played in unison with the guitar on a Jaymar toy piano from the 70's. I found the little piano in a secondhand shop on Sunset [Boulevard] and originally wanted to get it for my little daughter. I was just mucking around with it in the studio when Greg heard it, and was so taken by the sound that he immediately wanted to record it. *Sebastian Padotzke*

This is really the Walter Mitty song, as the song wish suggests I do like to dream and sometimes when things get too much I tend to drift off into a fantasy world where "it's all good!"
I don't like couch critics who are not prepared to be a part of the change, "the big man" in the song is reality and we can't avoid it. It would be sometimes nice to be the observer from high above but I believe that position has been filled so we should make do with what we have, it's not that bad after all!! *Rea*

Fotografie: Olaf Heine

STARSHIP

run   and still you want to hide   and still you think your   star-ship's wait-ing out - side   you think that you can

run   you think that you can hide   you think that you've been   liv-ing such a beau-ti-ful   life   but there's no place to

run   no there's no place to   hide   you think that you can   dis-ap-pear from this world   I'm look-ing in your

eyes   I see that you're sur - prised   well ba - by there's no   star - ship wai-ting out-side

D.S. al Coda

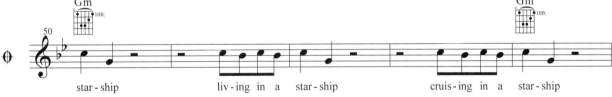

star - ship   liv-ing in a   star - ship   cruis-ing in a   star - ship

I'm liv - ing in   a   star-ship

BASS

Intro

etc. ad lib.

Samples

F-/Eb-Part 1

langsam abdämpfen

Bridge

A-Saite

In der Bridge wird die Basslinie immer mehr ver-dichtet. Die letzten 2 Durchgänge werden durch-gängig geachtelt, der letzte Durchgang eine Oktave tiefer auf der E-Saite gespielt. Ich habe „Starship" mit einem alten Fender Precision (60er Jahre) eingespielt, Round-Wound-Saiten 45 auf 105er Stärke, alter Ampeg SVT-Head, 8x10" Ampeg-Cabinet.

Alle Artikulationen müssen EXTREM gespielt werden: Stakkato muss fast eine Dead-Note sein, also extrem kurz. Haltebogen heißt wirklich, dass die Note wirklich bis zur nächsten gebunden wird. Die gesamte Bassline muss wie eine Scat-Gesangslinie klingen. Nur dann bekommt sie ihren besonderen Reiz. *Philipp Rauenbusch*

In the bridge the bass line is increasingly compact. The last two times through the line is played as eighths, and on the last time through an octave lower, played on the E string. I played 'Starship' with an old 60's Fender Precision, using round-wound strings (45 -105 gauge), an old Ampeg SVT head driving an 8x10" Ampeg cab.

All the articulations have to be played EXTREME-LY: that means that staccato has to be almost a dead note, really short. Tie means that the note really has to be held right up to the next one. The entire bass line has to be played to sound like a scat vocal – only then does it win its particular charm. *Philipp Rauenbusch*

Bei diesem Song wurde die Idee quasi aus dem Sound geboren. Das Preset 23 (Reslead) auf dem alten Roland JX8-P ist so starship like und 80er Jahre, dass der erste Jam des Songs in Irland in Rea's Studio eigentlich nur Spaß war. Das Demo aus Irland war dem späteren Song allerdings sehr ähnlich. Nur der Mittelteil kam später im Proberaum in L.A. dazu. *Sebastian Padotzke*

The idea for this song was born out of a sound - preset 23 ('reslead') from a vintage Roland JX8-P. It's just so spacey and 80's that when we first jammed the song in Rea's studio in Ireland, it was pretty much just for a laugh. However it turned out that the demo resembles the song in its later form very closely – it's only the middle section that was added during the LA rehearsals. *Sebastian Padotzke*

Roland YX8P - Preset "P23 - Reslead"

Fotografie Oliver Look

Fotografie Olaf Heine

Fotografie Olaf Heine

SERPENTINE

The song was written for arenas, sounds cocky I know but as a teenager I walked the stages of the world playing to the masses, it was difficult having my mum wake me and have to go to school but when it comes to writing you tend to slip into the subconscious and there lie the traces of teenage fantasy! This song supports the underlying theme of the album "No one can stop us from reaching who said the innocent survive!" basically saying we all get the chance and how high you shoot for is your own decision. The girl in the song is the dream and "Can't let her slip away".

I am beginning to sound like a hippie but it took me a long time to realise that fantasy and reality are not so far apart from each other. *Rea*

Fotografie: Olaf Heine

SERPENTINE

Fotografie: Olaf Heine

PROMISE

This is also a very simple song of two people believing enough in each other to survive the hard times. When we were recording in LA my wife was pregnant with our first baby and it wasn't sure if I would make the birth, it was a real hard time for us both, we were lucky to have iChat which meant we could at least see each other twice a day for an hour or so. My wife is a tough girl, small in build big in character, she never gave me a hard time about being away, and that she had to go through the pregnancy on her own and I will always be grateful to her for that. Promise is about making sure that the important things stay in focus and that the unimportant things become, as they should be unimportant. In true Hollywood style the end of the story was that I left on the 5th of November, landed on the 6th and our daughter was born on the 7th. *Rea*

Fotografie Olaf Heine

PROMISE

Bei „Promise" kam uns irgendwann im Proberaum die Idee, dieses Riff auf der Orgel durch den gesamten Song zu spielen. Obwohl ich das beim Aufnehmen bitter bereut habe, so war es doch ein Element, das dem Song die Tür zum Album geöffnet hat. So sieht das aus: *Sebastian Padotzke*

On 'Promise' the idea came to us in rehearsals to play the riff on the organ all the way through the song. Although I bitterly regretted doing it while recording, it turned out to be an element that acts a door in opening the album. This is how it looks: *Sebastian Padotzke*

Fotografie: Oliver Look

SHE'S A BOMB

This song is about one of my seven sisters, as it is not just complimentary but also critical I won't go into detail, needless to say she could walk into a room and ignite the atmosphere. She is a beauty queen with a tendency to terrorise. *Rea*

Fotografie: Olaf Heine

SHE'S A BOMB

D.S. al Coda
(without repeating)

31

KEYS

Der Bass kommt von der Korg Orgel (CX-3), nur die unteren 4 Register voll gezogen, den Drive offen und das Ganze durch einen Sansamp etwas verzerrt. *Sebastian Padotzke*

The bass comes from a Korg CX-3 organ, with just the lower four stops fully drawn, the drive on and then overdriven using a Sansamp.
Sebastian Padotzke

Fotografie: Rea

Fotografie: Oliver Look

TONIGHT

This is a song, which we had decided not to put on the album, we had left the recording studio (Sound City, LA) and had set up camp at Sound Factory, where we were mixing the album when we received a visit from our management and the record company boss. They both came in their own words to say hello and basically petition us to record a song they found amongst the demos, which they couldn't get out of their heads.

We were getting bored sitting around when Greg (Producer) was mixing and set up a small rehearsal room in the storeroom and decided to see if there would be 12 or 13 songs on the album. Now the truth is that as a band we are pretty difficult when it comes to listening to people's opinion about our music (while in the recording process), but the people who had travelled across half the world to convince us to record a song we loved but didn't know where to put on the album we decided to give it a go and see what happened.

We must have played the song 50 times the day we recorded it until eventually the statement... "Sounds like a record to me .." came from the control room. This was Greg's way of letting us know we had it in the bag. The song is about wanting something you can't have. I think there is a certain beauty in temptation, how it tries to convince you that it is the right thing to do even though you know it's not. *Rea*

Fotografie: Olaf Heine

TONIGHT

Fotografie Olaf Heine

Eines Tages kam bei unserem Studio ein ziemlich kaputter Typ vorbei (die Sorte, bei der man sofort sieht, dass er mehr erlebt hat als man selbst erleben muss, naja, ihr wisst schon was ich meine). Eine Sache, die ihn sehr sympathisch machte, war, dass er die Ladefläche seines Pick-up Trucks voller Gitarren und Verstärker hatte. Ich habe ein paar Sachen angespielt und habe mich dabei bis über beide Ohren in eine 69er Blonde Telecaster verliebt, die dann auch ziemlich schnell in meinen Besitz überging. Jedenfalls ist es diese Gitarre und mein 64er Fender Blackface Twin, den ihr bei diesem Song hört. Die Urversion von dem Song hatte einen spanischen Touch und war zum Verrücktwerden romantisch (diese Demoversion könnt ihr auf der „Tonight"-Single hören). Für das Album wollten wir aber eine Version entwickeln, die stilistisch besser zu dem passt, was sonst so auf dem Album passiert. Mit der Tele und dem Blackface bewaffnet, bin ich dann zu den Jungs in den Proberaum marschiert und wir haben den Song komplett umgekrempelt zu der genialen Version, wie ihr sie auf dem Album hören könnt. Ich liebe den Sound dieser Aufnahme. *Uwe Bossert*

One day we were in the studio and this guy came by. He looked pretty rough, you could see straight off that he'd been through stuff that you don't really need to go through yourself – you can probably guess what I mean. Anyway, he turned out to be a friendly sort, and importantly, had his pick-up sitting outside - stuffed to the gills with guitars and amplifiers. I gave a couple of things a quick try out and fell in love with a '69er Blonde Telecaster. I was quickly able to strike a good deal and voilà - there it is with my '64 Fender Blackface Twin on this song. The original version of this track had a Spanish touch, giving it a very romantic feel. For the album however we wanted a version that fitted better into the album as a whole. Armed with the Tele and the Blackface I marched into the rehearsal room and we turned the song around into the brilliant version you can now hear on the album. I love the sound of this recording. By the way, that original demo version I mentioned can be found on the 'Tonight' single. *Uwe Bossert*

KEYS

In diesem Song gibt es zwei Korg-Orgeln, eine Hammond B3 und einen Flügel. Da der Flügel mit der Gitarre unisono mitspielt, hier nur die zwei Orgeln, die sich mal abwechseln und mal ergänzen. *Sebastian Padotzke*

In this song there are two Korg organs, a Hammond B3 and a grand piano. Because the grand plays in unison with the guitar, here there are just the two organs that in part alternate and in part complement each other. *Sebastian Padotzke*

Fotografie Olaf Heine

JUST ANOTHER NIGHT

This is Greg's favourite song on the album, it is a very emotional song. It is really driven by the live atmosphere that was there when we recorded it. I was a bit of the weak link while recording as I was playing acoustic and kept on making stupid mistakes. I had to learn to find a flow where my guitar playing and singing harmonised. It sounds a bit stupid but when you go to record an album the things that were taken for granted like playing guitar and singing become such an obstacle. I spent ages trying to get back to the point where I forgot the mic's and the cables and the headphones and just played it. The last recording was the one we took the text "She racing through the crowd..." became such a vivid picture I felt I was living the song.

The song is about a strength I have seen in women that I not only respect but love, I had this picture of a girl who had been dumped and instead of falling into a slump she gives the world the bird and screams that she is stronger than the hurt. *Rea*

Fotografie: Oliver Look

JUST ANOTHER NIGHT

GIT

Ein ganz besonderer Song auf dem Album. Bei diesem Song haben wir den magischen Moment erwischt – alle zusammen in einem Raum und voll abgerockt. Deswegen haben wir uns auch dafür entschieden, kleinere Fehler nicht auszubessern, da alles was man an dieser Aufnahme verändert hätte, sie schlechter gemacht hätte. Dieser Song erinnert mich an die Anfänge unserer Bandgeschichte, so klingen wir im Proberaum!!! *Uwe Bossert*

A very special song on the album. On this track we managed to nail a very magical moment, namely all of us together in one room, rocking out to the max. Because of that we decided not to iron out the small mistakes – tampering with this recording would have only taken away something. This song reminds me of how the band started out. This is how we sound in the rehearsal room!!! *Uwe Bossert*

Fotografie: Olaf Heine

STARTING TO LIVE

I have always been someone who loves the aftermath, when the fight for what you want to achieve is over and you have got to where you want to be there is a certain sense of relief, success, and power. The adrenaline rush is something I live for, speed is a lifestyle and when you feel like you have the tempo under control a certain power races through your veins a certain sense of invincibility. Eventually you feel the instability everything shakes, you start to loose control you slow down and feel the rush resolve itself, stability sets in and a sense of release you feel you're starting to live! *Rea*

Fotografie: Olaf Heine

STARTING TO LIVE

D.S. al Coda

Bridge
oh   you feel like you're in o - ver - drive_____

oh   your shoot-ing stars_____ pass you by   you feel you're start - ing to live

Instrumental

oh_____

Bridge
_____ you feel like you're in o - ver - drive_____

oh   your shoot-ing stars   pass you by_____ you feel you're start - ing to

live   you feel you're loos-ing con - trol   you on-ly get what you   give

so let the che-mi-cals flow   yeah you're loos-ing con - trol____   a che-mi-cal

flow   it's   just   a   che - mi - cal

Bei diesem Song habe ich den jtm45 unseres Produzenten genommen und alle Regler bis zum Anschlag gedreht. Das war genau der Sound, den ich für diesen Song wollte. Dann gibt es einen kurzen Soloteil nach dem zweiten Refrain, wo wir nicht wirklich wussten was wir da machen wollten. An einem der letzten Aufnahmetage habe ich mich dann mit unserem Studioassistenten „Fig" und ein paar Sixpacks im Studio eingeschlossen und alles Mögliche ausprobiert. Was ihr jetzt an der Stelle hört, ist meine Les Paul und das „Burnvictim" (ein jcm800 100watt Topteil, das vor rund zehn Jahren aus einem brennendem Haus von einem Freund unseres Produzenten herausgeholt wurde und übel aussieht – sehr übel – deswegen „Burnvictim").

Um diesen Endlos-Sound hinzubekommen, habe ich die Line mit einem Ebow gespielt, zusätzlich habe ich ein Whammy und ein Delay verwendet. Wenn ihr mal einen Ebow verwendet, werdet ihr feststellen, dass man zwischen zwei Einstellungen wählen kann, in dem Solo hört ihr genau, wie ich diesen Schalter bewege. Nämlich genau nach dem ersten Drittel des Solos, wo die Line plötzlich viel mehr Obertöne bekommt und schärfer wird. Ebow muss man als Gitarrist mal in der Hand gehabt haben!! *Uwe Bossert*

Fotografie: Olaf Heine

For this song I used the producer's Marshall JTM45 with all the pots set to flat out – that was exactly the sound I wanted to get for this track. There's a short solo part after the second chorus where we hadn't got a clue what we should do there. Then one day shortly before we were to finish recording I locked myself away in the studio with Fig, the studio assistant and a couple of six packs, and tried out everything possible. What you can now hear at that point is my Les Paul and a JCM 800 100W head that earned the name 'the burn victim' after it was rescued from the burning house of a friend of the producers about ten years ago. I tell you, it looked (as opposed to sounded) bad – real bad. The nickname wasn't for nothing!

In order to get that infinite sound I played the line with an e-bow, additionally using a Whammy and a delay. If you've ever played with an e-bow then you know there are two settings you can choose between, and in the solo you can hear exactly how I switch between them – namely exactly after the first third of the solo, where the line suddenly gains a number of harmonics and becomes sharper. As a guitarist, you just have to have gotten your hand on an e-bow! *Uwe Bossert*

KEYS

Fotografie Olaf Heine

L.A. SKIES

This is a song about not thinking about tomorrow, we travel a lot and sometimes you're packing the same day you're unpacking. Living a dream is something that is difficult to explain but I have learned you have to live everyday for itself you can't be thinking about what's to come because then you miss out on what is happening now. As a musician you get used to leaving I'm not complaining I love my life but sometimes it's hard for those close to you, I tend to describe it as the start of the journey home. *Rea*

Fotografie Olaf Heine

L.A. SKIES

it feels right   we have got   to-day   we have got   to-night

and it feels   right

Fotografie Olaf Heine

SOMETIMES

This is a real dark song that eventually makes its way out of the darkness and into the light, you can get caught in the trap of asking yourself why things don't always go your way, after a while you feel like a magnet for anything that goes wrong. Eventually you realise that you are the only one who decides what happens to you, being sceptic is one thing waiting for the fall is another. In the song there is a moment when she turns her back on the hopelessness and "stands up and looks them straight in the eyes..." and starts again. We all deserve the chance to better ourselves to reach for the dream and to succeed, Sometimes the only one stopping you is yourself. *Rea*

Fotografie: Olaf Heine

SOMETIMES

Das Klavier ist ein uralter Steinway Flügel, der schon Jahrzehnte im Sound City steht. Elton John hat ihn umbauen lassen und ihm eine riesige hölzerne Haube verpasst, unter dem die Mikrofone eingebaut sind. So kann man live mit anderen recorden und hat trotzdem noch etwas Raum auf dem Flügel. Der Arpeggio-Sound ist ein alter Moog-„Roque", den ich durch ein altes Roland Space-Echo Tape-Delay geschickt habe. *Sebastian Padotzke*

The piano is an ancient Steinway grand that has been standing around Sound City for decades. Elton John had it modified, giving it a huge wooden 'bonnet' under which the microphones are placed. As such, you can record live with other instruments simultaneously and still capture some reverb on the grand. The arpeggio sound is an old Moog 'Roque' which I then put through a Roland Space Echo tape delay. *Sebastian Padotzke*

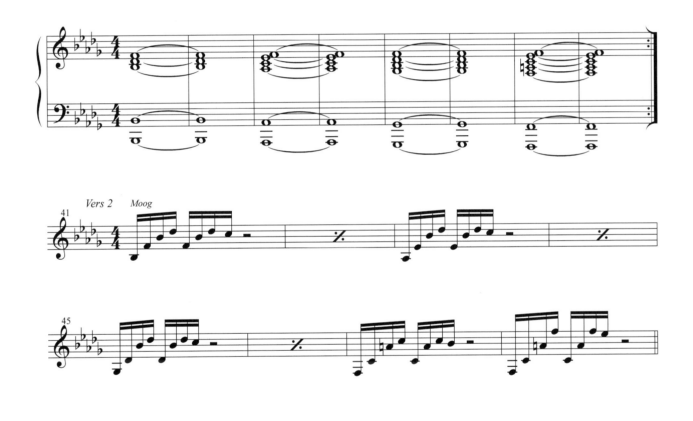

GIT

58

COME TO ME

This song touches on the theme of temptation again but rather than the beautiful side the hard reality to making the wrong choice. I have always believed you can fall and you can rise, come to me is the beckoning of some one to make the right decision and avoid the fall. I left Dublin in '98 one of the reasons was the fear of taking the fall, I had lost friends through drugs and felt I was getting sucked into their world, I felt by leaving like I was pulling myself out of the mire. Having found my way I sometimes look back on those times and wish I could have been more to those who didn't ever get to rise the truth is I wanted to be there for them like many had been there for me. *Rea*

Fotografie: Olaf Heine

COME TO ME

Fotografie: Olaf Heine

This song was written in the front sitting room of Sebi's house in Freiburg during a song writing session. We played it once and it never changed, the text and the music fell from the sky into our laps and every attempt to change it felt like a step in the wrong direction. In my opinion it is the first time in 4 albums that we touched on Irish folk music, the art of storytelling is something I have always loved and hope that this song in someway pays homage those who do it best. *Rea*

Fotografie: Olaf Heine

OUT OF REACH

KEYS

Der Song hat sich vom ersten Mal im Proberaum bis zum Album in seiner einfachen Art behauptet. Mit seiner Stimmung und seiner Melancholie ist er einer meiner Lieblingssongs auf diesem Album. Das Piano ist ein alter Steinway B-Flügel. Der Aufnahmeraum war bis auf das Piano leer, erhellt von hunderten von Grablichtern. *Sebastian Padotzke*

From the first run through in rehearsals to the album, the simple nature of this song made its presence felt. Because of its melancholic mood it belongs to one of my favourite songs on this album. The piano is an old Steinway B Grand. The room in which we recorded it was completely empty except for the piano, lit only by hundreds of candles. *Sebastian Padotzke*

Fotografie Oliver Look

Unglaublich geiler Song mit einer mega Atmosphäre. Hier konzentriert sich alles auf den Gesang und das Klavier. Ab der zweiten Strophe hört ihr so einen „jammernden" Sound, den man auch für ein Cello oder Ähnliches halten könnte. Ist aber eine E-Gitarre. Den Sound habe ich mit einem Metallslide und einem Ebow hinbekommen, die ich natürlich gleichzeitig verwende. Ist zwar ein sehr unauffälliger Part, aber meiner Meinung nach einer der schönsten Gitarrenparts auf dem Album.

Uwe Bossert

A fantastic song with a mega atmosphere. Here everything is concentrated on the vocal and the piano. From the second verse you can hear a sort of 'wailing' sound that could be a cello or something similar... in fact it's an electric guitar. I achieved the sound using a metal slide and an e-bow together. It's pretty inconspicuous but in my opinion one of the loveliest guitar parts on the entire album.

Uwe Bossert

Fotografie Olaf Heine

Fotografie: Olaf Heine

THE ONLY ONES

This song was always going to be the last song on the album, we knew that in the rehearsal room when we were doing the preproduction. It always had that feeling of the crowd leaving the venue, sweeping the floors locking the doors and turning off the lights. The text is about two people committed to each other and regardless what happens for every problem they will find the solution, it's a bit "Sonny and Cher" and "I got you Babe". *Rea*

Fotografie Olaf Heine

THE ONLY ONES

est of nights___ we'll be the on - ly ones_____ and if we hold on tight___

we'll make it through the night there's just you and me we are the on - ly ones

there's just you and me we are the on - ly ones

NEVER LETTIN' GO

This song was born, raised and laid to rest in Sound City studios LA *Rea*

NEVER LETTIN' GO

ooh_____ ooh_____ well I'm out
ooh_____ *D.S. al Coda*

I'm ne-ver let-ting go I looked a black - bird in the eyes and told

him what to say If he e-ver comes a-cross you on your way but I'm not

sure if black-birds real-ly know yeah I'm

spea-king to the spi-rits and the ghosts will talk a-gain some-one will save me this

ter-ri-ble pain with-out you_____ I'm all a-lone with-out you

but I'm ne-ver let-ting go I'm ne-ver let-ting go ooh_____

ENTSTEHUNGSGESCHICHTE

Die Entstehungsgeschichte dieses Songs ist recht ungewöhnlich ... Rea spielte im Studio etwas vor sich hin und Greg nahm es auf. Als Rea dann für ein paar Tage zu Hause war, um bei der Geburt seiner ersten Tochter dabei zu sein, haben Phil, Uwe, Sebi und ich diese Aufnahme mehr oder weniger zum ersten Mal gehört. Wir haben dann ohne Rea live dazu gespielt.

Nachdem er wieder bei uns war, brachte er seinen Part nochmals neu aufs Band und fertig war das Ding. Eine sehr spontane Nummer und einer meiner Favoriten der „Wish"-Session. Der Song hat es allerdings nicht aufs Album geschafft, weil wir das Gefühl hatten, dass er „etwas aus dem Rahmen fällt". Wer den Song trotzdem hören will, kann ihn z. B. auf der Vinylausgabe von „Wish" finden. *Gomezz*

The story of how this song came to be is pretty unusual. Rea played something in the studio and Greg recorded it. Rea then went home for a couple of days to be there for the birth of his daughter. It was at this point that Phil, Uwe, Sebi and I heard the recording properly for the first time. We then played live along to Rea without him being there!

After he returned he rerecorded his part and then it was finished. It's a very spontaneous track and one of my favourites from the 'Wish' session. The song didn't make it to the album in the end however because we had a feeling that it didn't quite 'fit in'. But you can still get to hear it on the vinyl version of 'Wish'. *Gomezz*

MOTHER EARTH

Mother Earth is a song about the world we live in and how we treat it. The truth is that we are running from a truth that like the world we live in if we keep running we will be confronted by the problem we are running from. I know the song didn't make it onto the album but I still feel it belongs to "Wish" as we loved the development and experiments we did during the recording of the song. For me the vocals were a lot of fun. There is a great reverb room in Sound City and we did some backing vocals that really added a twist in the background. When you hear them think of spaghetti westerns and the music that always accompanies the shoot outs in the film, Mother Earth was our "Fist Full of Dollars". *Rea*

Fotografie: Olaf Heine

MOTHER EARTH

„Mother Earth" ist ein weiterer Titel der „Wish"-Session, der es nicht aufs Album geschafft hat. Als wir die jetzige Songreihenfolge der Platte fertig hatten, waren wir alle begeistert. Es entstand nicht das Gefühl, dass dem Album noch etwas fehlt. Daher blieb dieser Song, wie schon „Never Lettin' Go", einfach „übrig". Wir wollten die Nummer allerdings nicht verschwinden lassen, weil wir sie alle sehr gut finden. „Mother Earth" ist bisher auf der Maxi von „Tonight" und auf der Vinyl-ausgabe von „Wish" veröffentlicht worden.

P.S: Es gab übrigens noch weitere Songs, an denen wir für „Wish" im Studio gearbeitet haben. Allerdings kamen wir nicht weit über das Aufnehmen der Basics hinaus. *Gomezz*

„Mother Earth" is another track from the 'Wish' session that didn't make it to the final album. Once we had reached the order of the songs on the album that eventually became the final tracklisting we were all very satisfied. There wasn't a feeling that something was missing, and for that reason, like 'Never Lettin' Go', 'Mother Earth' simply got 'left over'. We all liked the song however and as such it has so far been released as an extra track on the CD single version of 'Tonight' and on the vinyl edition of 'Wish'.

Just for the record (so-to-speak!) there were other songs that we worked on in the studio for possible inclusion on 'Wish', but these never got beyond the status of basic backing tracks. *Gomezz*

Fotografie Olaf Heine